SUPER
POWERS!

Raintree is an imprint of Capstone Global Library Limited, a company incorporated in England and Wales having its registered office at 264 Banbury Road, Oxford, OX2 7DY – Registered company number: 6695582

www.raintree.co.uk
myorders@raintree.co.uk

ISBN 978 1 4747 6662 3
22 21 20 19 18
10 9 8 7 6 5 4 3 2 1

British Library Cataloguing in Publication Data
A full catalogue record for this book is available from the British Library.

Editorial: Chris Harbo and Gena Chester
Design: Hilary Wacholz
Production: Kris Wilfahrt
Originated by Capstone Global Library Ltd
Printed and bound in India

Superman created by Jerry Siegel and Joe Shuster. By special arrangement with the Jerry Siegel family.

SUPER POWERS!™

Brimstone Attacks!

BY ART BALTAZAR AND FRANCO

a Capstone company — publishers for children

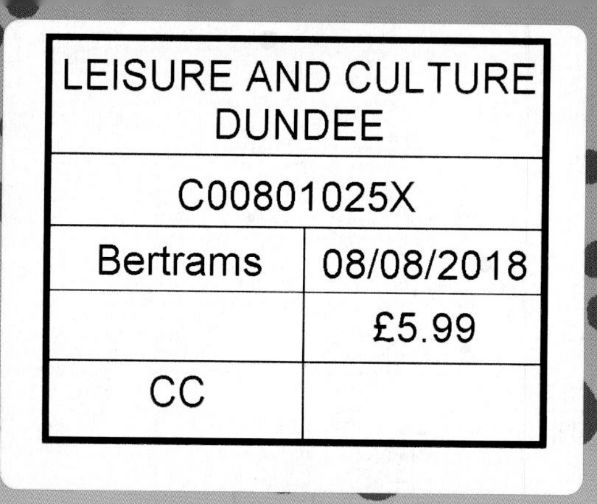

EVIL!
EVIL!
BLAH!
BLAH!
EVIL!
EVIL!
BLAH

MEANWHILE, IN METROPOLIS...
ALL IS PEACEFUL IN THIS PROGRESSIVE CITY...
DAILY PLANET
UNTIL...
A RUMBLING RUMBLES FROM DEEP UNDERGROUND...
SHAKE!
RUMBLE!
RUMBLE!
SHAKE!
RUMBLE!
UH-OH!
WHAT'S THIS SHAKING?
AW. THIS CAN'T BE GOOD!
WOOF!
AGAIN?
ONLY IN METROPOLIS!

SUPER POWERS!
BY ART BALTAZAR & FRANCO
WRITER & ARTIST
WRITER
KRISTY QUINN
EDITOR

JIMMY!
SNAP SOME PHOTOS!
THIS IS FRONT-PAGE NEWS!
RIGHT, MS. LANE!

RAAARGH!!!

ON SECOND THOUGHT...
...LET'S GET SOMEWHERE SAFE!
YEAH! GOOD IDEA!
DON'T WORRY, MS. LANE...

...I'LL CALL SUPERMAN FOR BACKUP!

NO NEED, JIMMY...
I GOT THIS!

SUPERGIRL!

STAND BACK, CITIZENS!

THIS LOOKS LIKE A JOB...

...FOR SUPERGIRL

NOW...
...IT'S TIME TO FIND OUT WHAT THIS IS ALL ABOUT!
WHY ARE YOU SO ANGRY, BIG GUY?

GRAB!

I AM BRIMSTONE!
I AM HERE TO CLEAR THE PATH FOR DARKSEID!

AND YOU CANNOT STOP ME!
TOSS!

OOF!

DID HE SAY...
...DARKSEID?
CLICK!

THAT BIG CREEPY STONE-FACED GUY WHO'S BEEN THREATENING TO TAKE OVER THE EARTH?
YEP.
THAT'S HIM!
IT'S A CRISIS

WHILE ON THE PLANET OF NEW KRYPTON...
WOW!
CONGRATS!
WHAT A BEAUTIFUL BABY BOY!
MEET YOUR NEW BROTHER...

...PRYM-EL!
RIME?
HE'S...
GREEN?
YES.
THE PHANTOM ZONE
DID THAT TO HIM.

AND HE
CAN FLY!

CONGRATULATIONS,
HALF BROTHER!
LOOKS LIKE WE ARE
ONE BIG HAPPY FAMILY,
EH, KAL-EL?

BACK IN METROPOLIS...
OH, NO!
METROPOLIS
OFFICER JOHN JONES
IS ON THE SCENE...
...WHILE FELLOW OFFICERS
CALL FOR MORE
POLICE BACKUP!

BRIMSTONE IS GETTING OUT OF CONTROL!
IT'S TIME I PROVIDE SOME BACKUP OF MY OWN!
OFFICER JONES IS SECRETLY...
THE MYSTERIOUS...
...MARTIAN MANHUNTER!

J'ONN!
I'M HERE TO HELP YOU, SUPERGIRL!

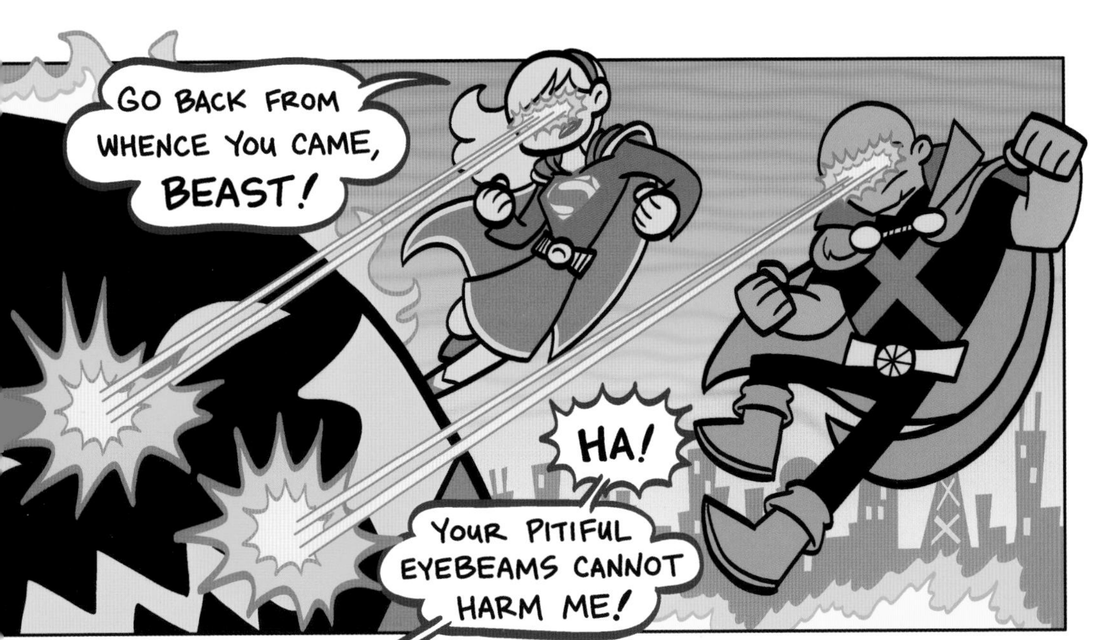
GO BACK FROM WHENCE YOU CAME, BEAST!
HA!
YOUR PITIFUL EYEBEAMS CANNOT HARM ME!

I QUITE ENJOY IT!
OUT OF MY WAY, FALSE HEROES!

NOW! FACE THE WRATH OF BRIMSTONE!
FFAAAHH!!

AAH! FIRE IS MY WEAKNESS!
YOU'LL BE SAFE UNDER MY SUPER-CAPE!

NOW! FOOLISH ONES!
PREPARE TO---

SQUIRT!

GET HIM, BOYS!

THANKS FOR THE PHONE CALL, MS. LANE!

READY! AIM! WATER!

REALLY?
OH, TINY HUMANS.
YOU ANNOY ME.

FWAAHH!

FREEZE BREATH

YOU!
WHAT DO YOU WANT, MARTIAN?

OW!
PUNCH!

A ROPE?
NICE.
I APPRECIATE YOUR EFFORTS.

AND YOU ARE...?

I AM WONDER WOMAN!
AND YOU WILL STOP THIS NONSENSE!

RIGHT.

YOU ARE WASTING YOUR TIME!

WHAT THE--?!
UNGOSHLY!
CLICK
HE MELTED THROUGH THE MAGIC LASSO!

EVIL! EVIL!
BLAH! BLAH!
EVIL! EVIL!
BLAH!

GRAB! GRAB!
HUH?

SWIPE!

THROW!

SPLASH!

WHAT'S UP, MY SURFACE FRIENDS?!
AQUAMAN!
I HEARD ABOUT THE HOT TIME YOU WERE HAVING UP HERE...
...AND I THOUGHT I'D COOL THINGS OFF A BIT!
IT'S ALL ABOUT TEAMWORK!
THANKS, AQUAMAN!
WHAT ABOUT BRIMSTONE?
OH, HE'S IN THE MIDDLE OF A TIME-OUT!
OH, C'MON GUYS!
CAN WE TALK ABOUT THIS?
OKAY... I GUESS I'LL HANG OUT HERE FOR A LITTLE WHILE.

MEANWHILE,
ON NEW KRYPTON...

PROUD DAY TODAY, EH, FATHER?
OH, HELLO, BRAINIAC.

Y'KNOW...
IT'S AMAZING...

...HOW MUCH OF OUR KRYPTONIAN TECHNOLOGY RELIES ON THESE CRYSTALS

WE ALL KNOW YOU WERE DESTROYED ALONG WITH PLANET KRYPTON.

MY SPIRIT LIVES ON, MY FRIEND.

IT'S FUNNY YOU MENTION THAT!

ZOD?
WAIT.
WHAT ARE YOU GUYS UP TO?

OUR SPIRIT BELONGS TRAPPED IN THE FORTRESS OF SOLITUDE...
...NOT HERE ON NEW KRYPTON!

SO LONG, JOR-EL!
NNOOO...

HAVE YOU GUYS SEEN MY DAD?
UM... JOR-EL?
NOPE.
DIDN'T SEE HIM.

DID YOU TRY CHECKING THE FORTRESS OF SOLITUDE?
HEH, HEH.

EARTH?
WHY WOULD HE BE ON...

KAL-EL!

SOMETHING IS HAPPENING TO PRYM-EL!
IS THERE A PROBLEM, MOTHER?
HE'S...
...GROWING!
WHAT? GROWING

HELLO, MOTHER.
HELLO, BROTHER.
HE JUST AGED SEVERAL YEARS IN ONE DAY!
OH.
CALL ME SUPERBOY PRYME!

PROLOGUE...

HA!
EXCELLENT.

WHAT IS IT, LUTHOR?
THE NEW KRYPTONIAN IS GROWING FAST, JUST AS PREDICTED.

EXCELLENT!
HE WILL BE THE KEY TO THE DESTRUCTION OF EARTH AND THE DEMISE OF THE JUSTICE LEAGUE!
SO SAYS DARKSEID OF APOKOLIPS!
HA HA HEE HOH!

CREATORS

ART BALTAZAR IS A CARTOONIST MACHINE FROM THE HEART OF CHICAGO! HE DEFINES CARTOONS AND COMICS NOT ONLY AS AN ART STYLE, BUT AS A WAY OF LIFE. CURRENTLY, ART IS THE CREATIVE FORCE BEHIND *THE NEW YORK TIMES* BEST-SELLING, EISNER AWARD-WINNING DC COMICS SERIES TINY TITANS, THE CO-WRITER FOR *BILLY BATSON AND THE MAGIC OF SHAZAM!,* AND CO-CREATOR OF SUPERMAN FAMILY ADVENTURES. ART IS LIVING THE DREAM! HE DRAWS COMICS AND NEVER HAS TO LEAVE THE HOUSE. HE LIVES WITH HIS LOVELY WIFE, ROSE, BIG BOY SONNY, LITTLE BOY GORDON AND LITTLE GIRL AUDREY. RIGHT ON!

FRANCO AURELIANI, BRONX, NEW YORK, BORN WRITER AND ARTIST, HAS BEEN DRAWING COMICS SINCE HE COULD HOLD A CRAYON. CURRENTLY RESIDING IN UPSTATE NEW YORK WITH HIS WIFE, IVETTE, AND SON, NICOLAS, FRANCO SPENDS MOST OF HIS DAYS IN A BATCAVE-LIKE STUDIO WHERE HE HAS PRODUCED DC'S TINY TITANS COMICS. IN 1995, FRANCO FOUNDED BLINDWOLF STUDIOS, AN INDEPENDENT ART STUDIO WHERE HE AND FELLOW CREATORS CAN CREATE CHILDREN'S COMICS. FRANCO IS THE CREATOR, ARTIST, AND WRITER OF *PATRICK THE WOLF BOY*. WHEN HE'S NOT WRITING AND DRAWING, FRANCO ALSO TEACHES HIGH SCHOOL ART.

GLOSSARY

brimstone old name for sulphur; a smell related to the eruption of volcanoes

citizen person who lives there in a country or city

crystal clear or nearly clear mineral or rock

demise unfortunate end

lasso length of rope with a loop at the end, usually used to capture animals

league group of people with a common interest or activity such as justice

Martian inhabitant of Mars

nonsense something silly, or that has no meaning

officer someone who is in charge of other people

prime of first importance or quality

progressive making use of or interested in new ideas

spirit ghost

surface outside or outermost area of something

teamwork people working together

weakness disadvantage

VISUAL QUESTIONS AND WRITING PROMPTS

1. WHY DO YOU THINK SUPERGIRL'S AND J'ONN'S LASER BEAM VISION DIDN'T WORK ON BRIMSTONE?

2. LOOK AT THE DEFINITION OF "BRIMSTONE" IN THE GLOSSARY. NOW LOOK AT THE CHARACTER BRIMSTONE BELOW. HOW DOES THE DEFINITION FIT THE EVIL VILLAIN?

3. WRITE A SCENE ABOUT JOR-EL WHILE HE'S TRAPPED IN THE FORTRESS OF SOLITUDE.

4. HOW DO YOU THINK LEX LUTHER AND DARKSEID ARE COMMUNICATING?

READ THEM ALL!

SUPER
POWERS!